CW00867345

THE FUNNY LIFE OF MILO:

Where is Mr. Nose?

J.S. HOLDAWAY
ILLUSTRATED BY NESI BUENCAMINO

Yesterday, I blew my nose...

Right off of my face!

And my nose started running
all around my place.

He was jumping on the couch,

And running down the hall.

And sliding down the wall.

He left a trail of snot.

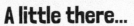

When I came back, he was gone.
But where did he go? The search was on!

Was he hiding in the kitchen?

on

and in.

Then I heard him sneeze again.

I chased him to the table
and across the kitchen floor.

But he just kept on running
and ran right out the door.

I told my runny nose to stop.

But my nose didn't listen well,
He was only made to smell.

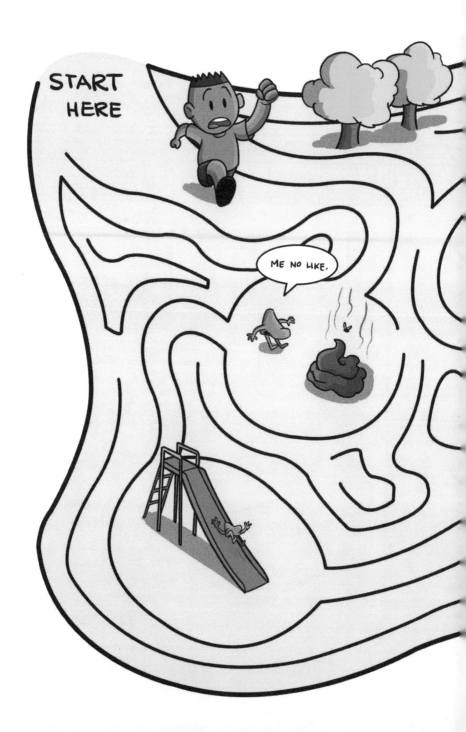

He didn't have ears to hear or eyes to see.
He was just a nose running free.

FINISH

Which is probably why he didn't get too far.
He couldn't see that speeding car.

And after that, my nose was flat.

"I see," he said. "Your snout is out? That's no reason for you to pout. I can fix all your woes. You just have to pick your nose."

"I can't pick my nose," I said. "I'm pretty sure my nose is dead."

"My mom can't pick my nose," I cried.
"Don't you listen? My nose died!"

"I know!" he said. "So come on in...or you'll never pick your nose again."

When I got to his office, I saw quite a sight.
It turns out the doctor was technically right.
Because there on his wall, hung row after row,
were all kinds of noses all ready to blow.

I saw ant-eater noses

and noses for moles.

I tried it on if it had two holes.

But I could choose only one...

And I think I chose well.
Do you like my new nose?
It does more than just smell!

The End.

Finally, you made it. Good job! It's over now. There's no more. That's it. The end. You can stop reading. Anytime now. Stop reading. The plot has reached a resolution. Milo has his nose. Everyone's happy.

Except the cat. He's never happy. And sometimes Milo. He's not always happy either. Like when his dad breaks wind. That was the one good thing about not having a nose. Wait, why are we still talking? You've already reached the end. Don't you have other things to do? Put the book down. Seriously.

And...you're still here. Okay, I've got an idea. Go to Amazon.com and write a review. Then check out Milo's other adventures.

Wow. Back already? Thinking... Thinking... Okay, new idea. Staring contest. Blink first and you lose. If I win, you have to close the book. Deal? It's my bedtime and I want to sleep. And I can't fall asleep if the book is open.

Are you ready? Three, two, one, GO! Staring Contest! Stare into my i's. iiiiiiiiiiiiiiiiiiiiiiiiiiiiii. Oops. Wrong kind of i.

Starting over. Staring contest in three, two, one GO! Stare into my Eyes. Eye. Eye. Eye. Eye. Eye. Eye. Eye. Eye. Eye. Eye. Eye. Eye. Eye. Eye. Eye.

Uh-oh, you blinked. I won! Good night! So long! Farewell. Adieu, Adieu, Adieu.

funnymilo.com

CPSIA information can be obtained
at www.ICGtesting.com
Printed in the USA
LVHW070805150722
723541LV00006B/40

9 781736 796948